THE BFG

FILM STORYBOOK

Based upon THE BFG, an original story by
ROALD DAHL

Pictures and story from the animated film by
COSGROVE HALL PRODUCTIONS

Designed by
BET AYER

PUFFIN BOOKS

PUFFIN BOOKS

Published by the Penguin Group
27 Wrights Lane, London W8 5TZ, England
Viking Penguin Inc., 40 West 23rd Street, New York, New York 10010, USA
Penguin Books Australia Ltd, Ringwood, Victoria, Australia
Penguin Books Canada Ltd, 2801 John Street, Markham, Ontario, Canada L3R 1B4
Penguin Books (NZ) Ltd, 182–190 Wairau Road, Auckland 10, New Zealand

Penguin Books Ltd, Registered Offices: Harmondsworth, Middlesex, England

First published 1989

Text and illustrations copyright © Cosgrove Hall Productions Limited, 1989

Typeset in Rockwell (Linotron 202) by
Rowland Phototypesetting (London) Ltd

Made and printed in Great Britain by
William Clowes and Sons Ltd, Beccles

One night at the witching hour, when everything was still, something very tall and very black began to creep over the countryside towards a sleeping village. An owl screeched in fright . . .

. . . and flew swiftly between the houses . . .

. . . towards the village orphanage.

THE CLONKERS HOME FOR GIRLS

All the children in the dormitory were asleep, except Sophie. She saw the owl settle on her skylight window.

She tiptoed out to look more closely. Then a voice from downstairs shouted:

Get back to bed! Punishment in the morning!

But Sophie was determined to look out on to the shimmering moonlit street. She had never seen it so beautiful and still.

Then, just as she was closing the curtains, something caught her eye.

What was that!?

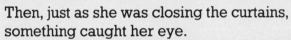

Suddenly the Giant swung round. He had seen her! Sophie jumped quickly back into bed, but it was too late.

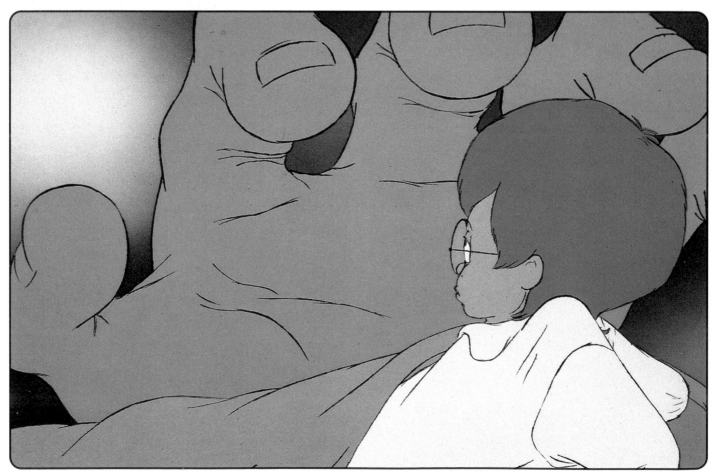

Before she knew it, he had dragged her out, blankets and all . . .

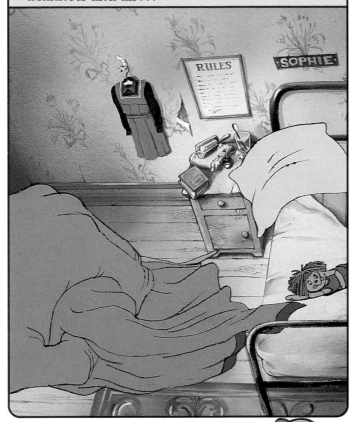

. . . carried her through fields and forests . . .

. . . and, with one enormous leap, up into the sky!

At last they landed in a strange, barren world. The Giant hurried into a cave inside a mysterious mountain.

"Now then, what has we got here?" roared the Giant. "I is hungry!"

"Please don't eat me," said Sophie.

"Of course I is not eating you," said the Giant. "I is eating snozz-cumber." And he cut himself a slice of a big, smelly, stripy vegetable.

"Don't Giants eat people then?" asked Sophie.

"Oh, yes!" shouted the Giant as he towered above her. "All the Giants round here is guzzling up yuman beans every night. They will swallow you up too if they catches one tiny glimp of you."

Sophie felt very unhappy at the idea. Then the Giant grinned a giant grin, which spread from one enormous ear to the other, and his blue eyes twinkled as he leaned over her. "But not me," he said. "I is not like all the others. I is a nice Giant. I is a freaky Giant. I is the Big Friendly Giant. The B-F-G, that's me!"

Sophie felt very much better.

"Does you have a name?" asked the BFG.

"Yes. My name's Sophie."

"Well, now," said the BFG. "Is you liking some supper, Sophie?"

He offered her a big lump of smelly snozzcumber, but it was so horrible she screwed up her face in disgust.

"It's all there is to eat round here," said the BFG, "if you is not eating yuman beans."

"You could get apples from the orchards near our village," suggested Sophie.

"Oh, no," said the BFG. "I does not go snitching things."

"Then why did you snitch me?" asked Sophie.

"Because people is not allowed to be seeing Giants. If I had not snitched you away, you would be telling everybody about me. Then they would come and capture me and put me in a zoo."

"Not if you didn't harm anybody," said Sophie. "Anyway, you're too big."

"Elefunts is big," said the BFG. "Elefunts does not harm anybody. Elefunts is captured and put in zoos."

"That's true," said Sophie.

"So you is just having to stay here with us," said the BFG. "Me and Humplecrimp."

And Sophie noticed a little animal which was nibbling greedily at the snozzcumber, despite its ghastly taste.

"You'll be safe with us," said the BFG.

But just as he said it, a gruesome monster, bigger even than the BFG, came roaring into the cave.

I smell yuman bean. Gimme.

Have some snozzcumber instead, Bloodbottler.

But the BFG did not know that Sophie had hidden inside it! The Bloodbottler crunched the snozzcumber in

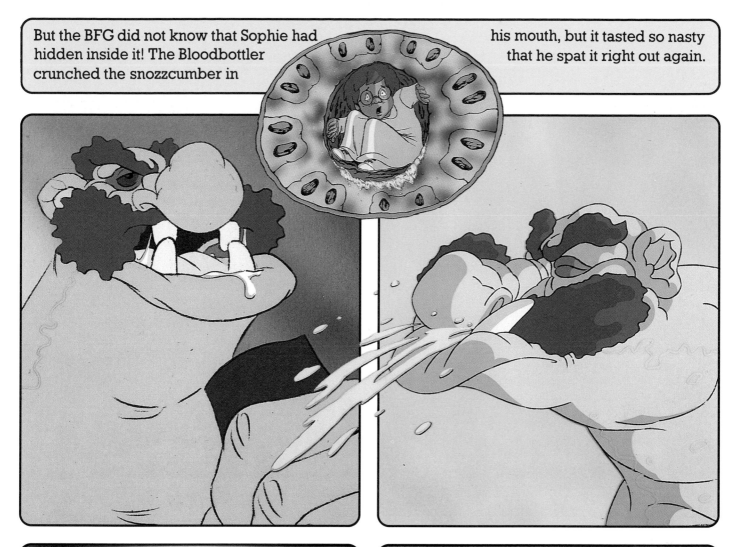

his mouth, but it tasted so nasty that he spat it right out again.

He screamed at the BFG and stormed out of the cave.

"Oh, Sophie," thought the BFG. "Where is you?"

Then he saw something moving in the corner.

I'm over here!

He nearly ate me up with the snozzcumber. It was horrible. I'm all smelly and sticky but I'm not hurt.

"I hope he didn't hurt *you*," said Sophie.
"Oh, no, I is as right as snow," replied the BFG...

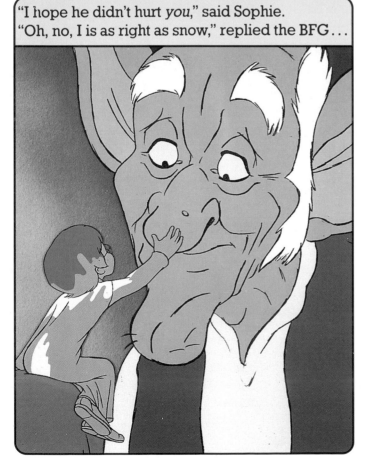

"... but you is needing a bath."

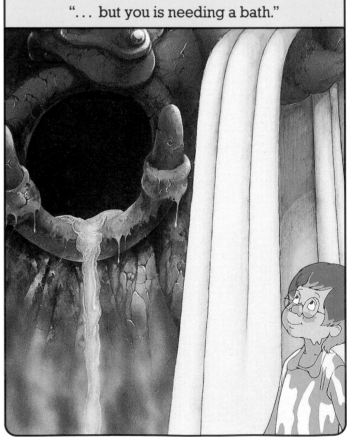

BFG, what were you doing in our village? I saw you blowing a trumpet.

I was blowing a dream. It's my job. I blows nice dreams to little chiddlers every night.

"Now, here is a new dress for you," said the BFG.

Oh! It's lovely!

Sophie was thirsty, but the BFG only had a curious drink called frobscottle.

Look, it's fizzing the wrong way! The bubbles are going down instead of up!

Well, if bubbles is fizzing upwards, they would come out in a foulsome, belchy burp. That is catasterous! Giants is never doing it.

But if bubbles are going *down*, they might come out . . . somewhere else. That would make a much worse noise, wouldn't it?

You is exuncly right. A whizzpopper! It's a sign of happiness. It is jollifying music.

It's not. It's very rude.

You yuman beans is making whizzpoppers. Everybody is. Try some.

It tastes fantastic!

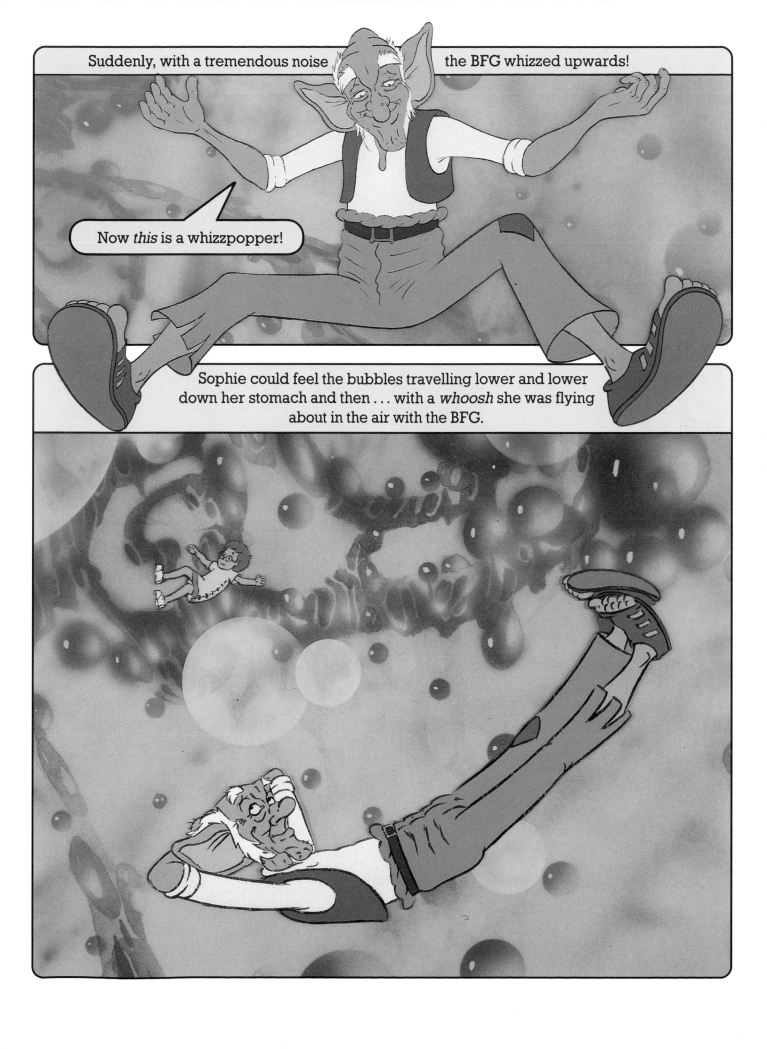

But it had been a long day. She floated down into the BFG's hands, fast asleep.

The next morning . . .

. . . the BFG got up early and put Sophie in his pocket.

Come on!
We're off to collect some dreams.

But first they had to get past the other Giants.

Suddenly the biggest Giant, the Flesh-lumpeater, grabbed the BFG.

Sophie was very frightened. But the terrible Giant threw the BFG down again with a bump.

They ran away as fast as they could...

...until they reached the Dreamway, the stairway to Dream Country.

The BFG packed his case and started the long journey home to Giant Country.

On the way they stopped by a pool.

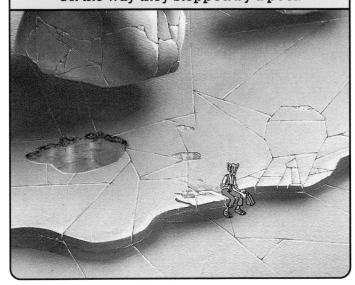

Sophie thought she would explore some stepping-stones.

But when she stepped on one – it moved! It was an enormous beetle, and it flew away with Sophie on its back.

Sophie gasped with relief when it put her down. But where was she?

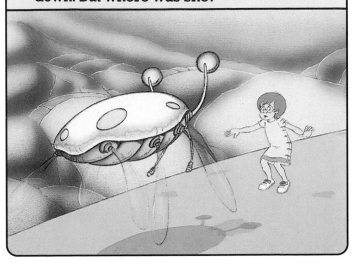

She was on a Giant's belly!

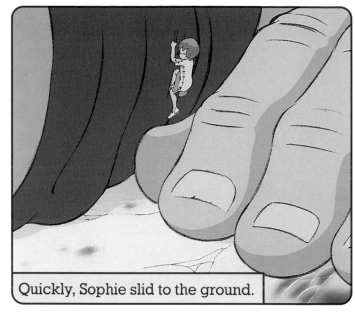

Quickly, Sophie slid to the ground.

But the Giants had smelt her!

Hiding behind a rock, Sophie tried to get her breath back.

Then, out of nowhere, a hand reached out and grabbed her!

It was the BFG. She was safe.

The BFG went to lock the trogglehumper away.

Now you won't be scaring any little chiddlers.

Then the BFG showed Sophie how he mixed dreams. She watched as he made a dream about a little boy who became invisible when he pressed his tummy button and then scared his algebra teacher by looking like a ghost.

"A boy would like that dream," said Sophie.

But the BFG was not the only Giant in the village that night . . .

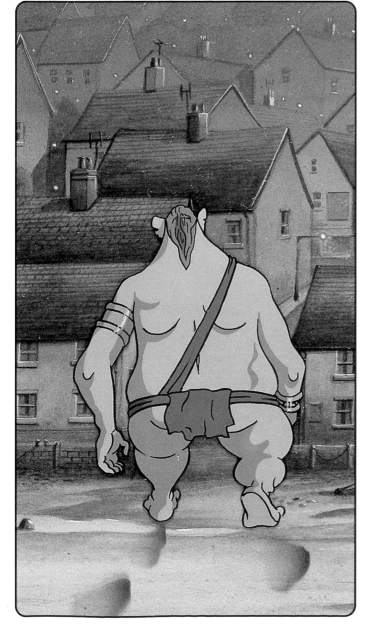

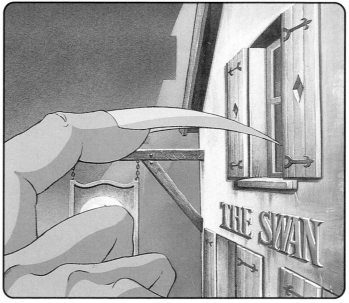

Hidden round the corner, Sophie saw what was happening and screamed.

No! Don't!

The Fleshlumpeater heard Sophie but when he turned round, the BFG had already whisked her away.

"You should have stopped him!" cried Sophie.
"There is no way of stopping any of the Giants," replied the BFG.
"There must be," said Sophie. "We'll get someone to help us."
"Who would help us?" said the BFG.
"There's the Queen of England. Yes, we'll go to the Queen."
"She'll never believe you in a month of Mondays," replied the BFG.
"We'll make her believe us."
"How?" asked the BFG gloomily.

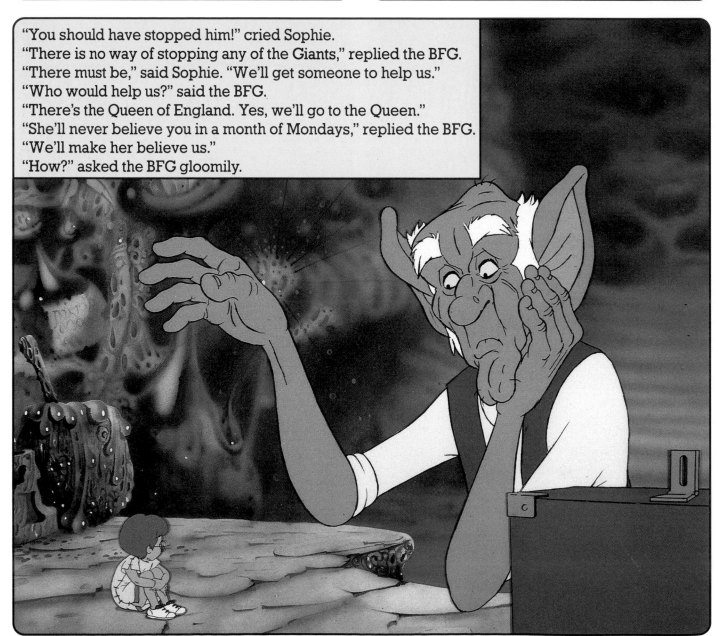

Then Sophie had an idea.

We'll blow a dream to the Queen. Come on, BFG.

The BFG began to mix a special dream.

I hope this is going to work.

I hope so, too.

Later that night, they arrived at Buckingham Palace.

Where is the Queen sleeping? This one is a lady. Take a look-see.

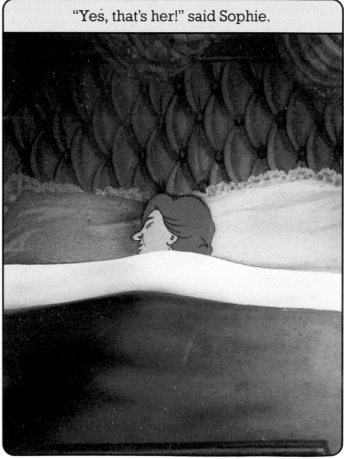

"Yes, that's her!" said Sophie.

Sophie climbed on the sill while the BFG blew the dream.

"Now we just have to wait," said the BFG

Grrr! Gobble them all up!

My name is Sophie.

Oh, Mary, I've had the most awful nightmare about Giants eating up little children.

"But it's true! It's in all the papers," replied Mary.

Then, as she went to open the curtains . . .

How did you get in here? Oh, you'll be for it, you will!

"But you were the girl in my dream," said the Queen, "and I dreamed a Giant brought you here."
"Yes, he's my friend, the BFG," said Sophie. "He's in the garden. Shall I call him?"

Your Majester, I is your humbug servant. I has great secrets to tell you.

I would be delighted to hear them. Would you care to join us for breakfast?

Later that morning in the ballroom the BFG, the Queen and Sophie were finishing their breakfast.

Tibbs, would you summon the head of the Army and the head of the Airforce? Tell them it's an emergency.

"Good morning, gentlemen. You have heard the dreadful news of the disappearing children?" asked the Queen.
"I'm sure there's a perfectly simple explanation Ma'am," answered the officers.
"There is. They were eaten by Giants," replied the Queen.

But Giants don't exist, Ma'am . . . er . . . do they?

Gentlemen, may I introduce Sophie? And this is our friend, Mr BFG.

But when the BFG stood up to salute . . .

Ow! What was that?

That *was* Louis XV.

Then, the BFG told them the whole story.

Good heavens, how many of these brutes are there?

Well, there's Manhugger, Meatdripper, Childchewer, Butcher Boy, Bloodbottler, Maid Masher, Fleshlumpeater, Bonecruncher, and the Gizzardgulper. That is . . . er . . . nine.

"We'll send in the tanks and the guns and the heavy artillery," said the head of the Army. "Dacca, dacca, dacca!"

"Piffle!" said the head of the Airforce. "We'll send planes with bombs and rockets. Pow! Kaboom!"

"Gentlemen," said the Queen. "There will be no guns and no bombs."

But how can we capture them without guns or bombs?

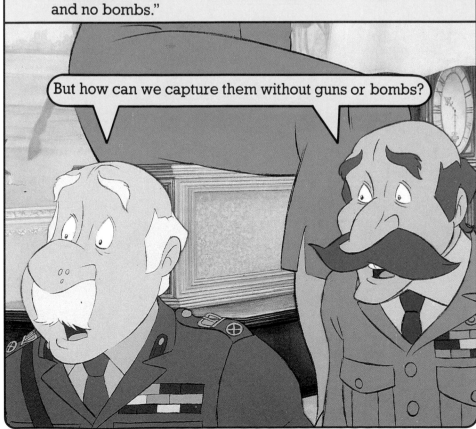

I know a way.

The next day the BFG and Sophie led a fleet of nine helicopters into Giant Country.

While the Giants slept, the men took up their positions . . .

. . . and tied the Giants up and hauled them away on their helicopters.

They've done it!

But everyone had forgotten the Fleshlumpeater!

ARGH!

We won't be needing the last helicopter, sir. There were only eight of them.

Sophie ran as fast as she could into the BFG's cave.

But the Fleshlumpeater followed smashing everything in his way.

Meanwhile the BFG picked himself up . . .

. . . and struggled towards the Dream Cave.

Then the Humplecrimp led Sophie into its hole.

But the Fleshlumpeater thumped his fist in rage from above . . .

. . . and Sophie was hurtled

through the tunnel until she

fell out the other end . . .

. . . and found herself face to face . . .

. . . with the Fleshlumpeater himself!

Sophie tried to run away.

Help!

It was too late! She was caught.

Meanwhile the BFG . . .

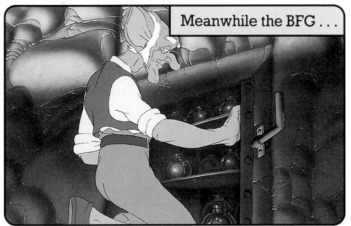

. . . rushed from the Dream Cave . . .

. . . and blew the terrible Trogglehumper into the Fleshlumpeater's face.

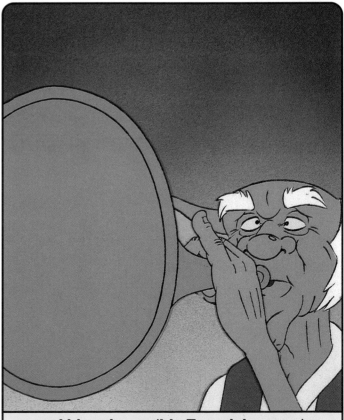

No! Jack! Leave me alone!

Oh, BFG, you saved me!

The Fleshlumpeater fell down outside the cave and was soon tied up like the other Giants.

Then they were all taken back to London . . .

. . . and dropped into a big pit where they were made to eat snozzcumbers.

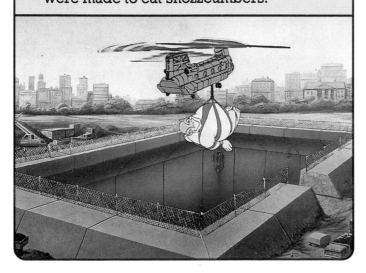

"What was the dream you blew him?" asked Sophie.

"It was about Jack," said the BFG. "Jack is the only thing all Giants is frightened of."

"Has he got a beanstalk?" giggled Sophie.

"Yes. I is very frightened of him," said the BFG.

"Well, you needn't be," said Sophie. "Remind me to tell you why one day."

At Buckingham Palace the Queen gave medals to everyone. She announced that Sophie and all the other little girls from Mrs Clonker's horrible orphanage could live in her palace for ever. And to the BFG she gave the biggest royal castle in England to be his home.

Thank you, Majester, but I cannot be staying. I must be tootling off now.

You're not going?

You're not going?

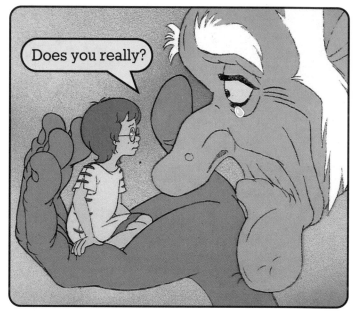

And they flew off together back to Giant Country and new adventures.

THE END